Hoot and Peep
A Song for Snow

Lita Judge

Dial Books for Young Readers

It was Peep's first winter, and she cuddled close to her big brother, Hoot.

"Brrr, the air is crisp tonight," said Hoot. "Snow will come soon."

"SNOW?"
said Peep.

"When will she get here?"

"Snow isn't a *she*, Peeps. Snow is a frozen thing that falls from the sky. Trust me, you'll like it. I'll show you the best place to wait for snow."

"Rain falls from the sky," said Peep.
"Does snow drop, ploppety splop,
like the rain's song?"

"Does it
swish swooooooo
like the wind's song?"

"Does it **scrrinkle scrattle** like falling leaves?"

"Hooo," answered Hoot. He kept his answer vague because he couldn't remember snow's song. He was only Peep's age when he saw it the winter before.

"Snow is cold, Peeps." He did remember that much.

"Here, you are littler than me.
You'll need this."

"Snow snow snow. Snow is cold, snow is . . ." Peep didn't know how to finish her song for snow.

"What are you doing now?" asked Peep.

"Waiting for snow," said Hoot.

"Why isn't snow here yet? You said it would come!"

"It will," said Hoot.

"I don't believe you. I think you just made it up," said Peep.

"Ah, Peeps. Try to have some owly patience," said Hoot.

Peep decided to go find snow herself.

She went to ask Squirrel if he had seen the snow. He hadn't. It was his first winter, too.

But he did have his own song
that Peep could sing.

"Schweepity
peep,
chickity
choot."

"Chick, chica,
choot."

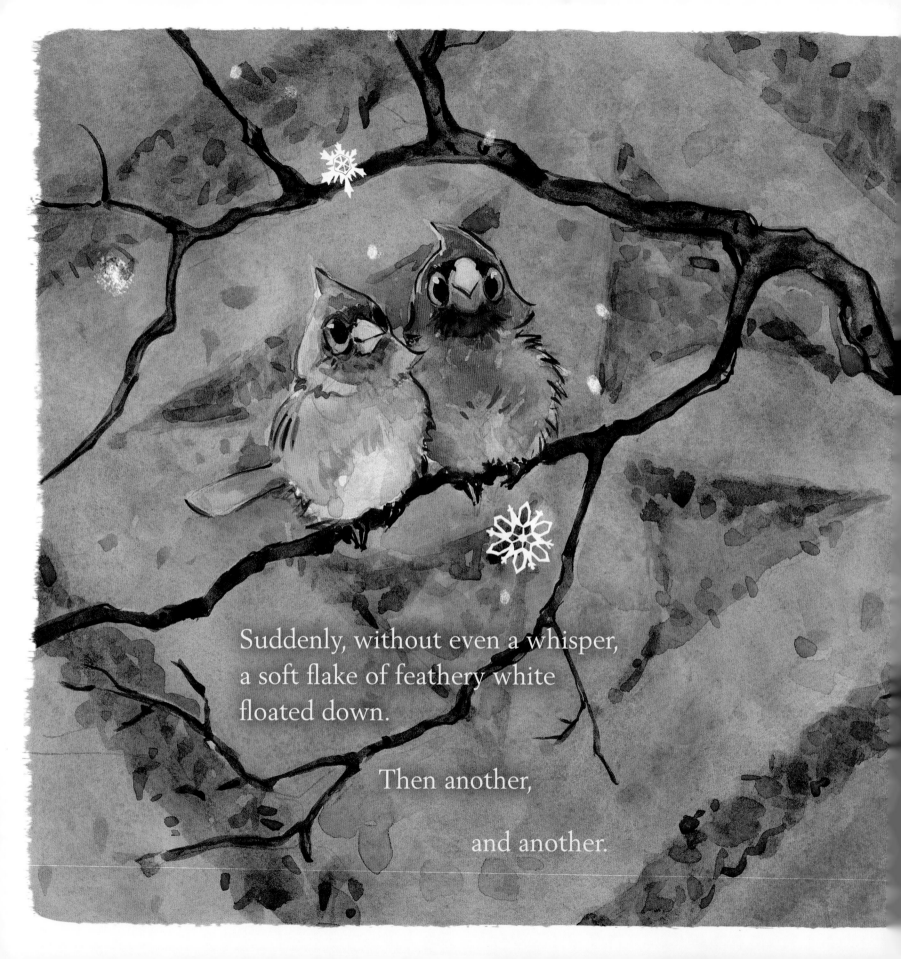

Suddenly, without even a whisper,
a soft flake of feathery white
floated down.

Then another,

and another.

The night sky filled
with sparkly white.

"Snow is here!" said Hoot.

Peep realized how wise her big brother had been to wait quietly to welcome the snow.

"Snow's song is silence,"
Peep whispered.

"Hoooo," agreed Hoot.

Hoot and Peep watched as
the green bushes, brown trees,
and gray stone turned into a
soft world of white.

"How do we sing along with snow?" asked Peep.

"We can make up our own snow songs," said Hoot.

"Hooooooo," sang Hoot.

"Scwheeee,"

sang Peep.

Thwump!

"I know another song for snow," said Peep.

"Schweepity thwap, thwap."

"Hooo!" said Hoot.
It wasn't his favorite
snow song.

"Schweep," said Peep as she wrapped Hoot in pretty lights. It was her best way of saying *I'm sorry*.

"That's okay, little Peeps."

Thwap

Hoot and Peep played
as the sun crept soundlessly
into the violet sky.

Morning light sparkled on the snow,
and the little owls grew sleepy.
Then they curled up together,
and sang softly to each other,
a song of good night.

DIAL BOOKS FOR YOUNG READERS
Penguin Young Readers Group
An imprint of Penguin Random House LLC
375 Hudson Street | New York, New York 10014

ISBN 9781101994511

Manufactured in China on acid-free paper
10 9 8 7 6 5 4 3 2

Design by Jennifer Kelly
Text set in Berling LT Std

*The illustrations were created using watercolors
with a few digital finishing touches.*

For Dave, my Hoot

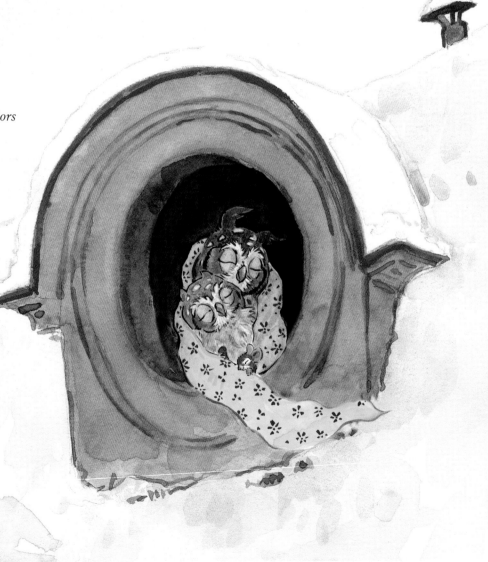